SU SU

GABBY

TIMOTHY

GATOR

FLEX

HENRIETTA

CHAPTER 1

KAYNE'S WORLD

LC turned his knapsack upside down and dumped everything into a pile on the living room rug. He pushed his notebook and pencils off to one side. Then he carefully picked up the two rookie baseball cards he had traded with his best friend, Tiger, for fifty cents. He was sure they were worth a dollar each. It was a great trade. Probably the best trade he'd ever made.

At the bottom of the pile was a

half-chewed piece of Bananarama gum,
two green-and-yellow marbles, and half a
peanut butter and marshmallow sandwich
he had forgotten to eat for lunch. The sandwich was stuck to the bottom of his knapsack. There was white marshmallow goop

all over the inside of his knapsack.

LC flopped on his stomach and propped his head on his hands. He didn't like to do his homework in his room. He liked to do it lying on the floor in the living room. He could think better that way.

LC opened his math book to the page he had to do for homework. Luckily, it was only a little bit sticky.

TRAIN A is heading west going 20 miles per hour (MPH). TRAIN B is heading east going 32 miles per hour. In 2 hours and 15 minutes the two trains will meet. How many miles will TRAIN A have traveled? TRAIN B?

LC picked up his favorite pencil. He thought word problems were the worst. Numbers were bad enough, but numbers with words were totally wack.

LC drew a picture of a railroad track. Then he drew a picture of TRAIN A and wrote "20 MPH" under it. Then he drew a picture of TRAIN B crashing into TRAIN A.

"*Craaaasssshhhh!!!*" LC said. "A major

head-on collision. No survivors."

LC bit the end of the pencil and started to chew the eraser. He tried to figure out how far TRAIN A might have traveled. But it was no use. He was completely stuck. He looked down at his watch. Maybe he could use his stopwatch to figure it out.

"Four o'clock," LC said. "It's time for

KAYNE'S WORLD."

LC knew he wasn't supposed to watch TV. But he would only do it for a minute. Nobody would know.

He looked around. The coast was clear. He grabbed the TV remote control, lowered

the volume, and turned on the TV to his favorite channel—**CTV**.

LC was only allowed to watch **CTV** on the weekend. But he figured a minute wouldn't hurt. Kayne was the coolest dude. Everybody in school watched **KAYNE'S WORLD**.

Kayne was on a beach with a bunch of surfer kids. LC turned up the volume just a little. LC loved surfing. He had to hear what Kayne was saying.

KAYNE: *Hey, dudes! Gnarly! Rad! We're here at Big Surf Beach, the coolest beach with the baddest waves.*

LC turned the volume up more. He couldn't miss a word. He planned to be a champion surfer one day.

KAYNE: *And this weekend we're going to have the most jammin', slammin', rippin', surfing competition ever—and you're all invited—it's an open invitational. So come on down, dudes. And par-ty!*

"Wow!" LC exclaimed, sitting

up and pushing his math homework out of the way. "I gotta go."

"LC, are you doing your homework?" LC's mother called from the kitchen. "Is Little Sister in there with you?"

LC lowered the volume and pulled his homework in front of him.

"Noooo, I'm in my room doing my homework," Little Sister yelled from upstairs.

"Then what's all that noise?" Mrs. Critter asked.

"Nothing, Mom," LC said.

A few seconds later Little Sister walked into the living room. Before LC could say or do anything, she grabbed the remote and turned off the TV. "I knew you were watching **CTV**," Little Sister said. "I'm telling."

"You better not," LC said, trying to take the remote out of Little Sister's hands.

"I am so gonna tell," Little Sister said.

"Don't you dare," LC said, trying to grab the remote again.

"Weellll, what are you going to give me?" Little Sister asked.

"A piece of Bananarama gum?" LC said, picking up his old piece of gum.

"No way!" Little Sister said. "You already chewed it!"

"Only half of it," LC said. "Come on, Little Sister. You love Bananarama gum."

"Nope," Little Sister said. "Well, I guess I'll just have to tell." Little Sister stood very still and opened her mouth very wide. She was about to start yelling when LC jumped up and put his hand over her mouth.

"All right, you can have one of my lucky marbles," LC said, taking his hand off Little Sister's mouth.

"I don't want some dumb marble," Little Sister said.

"Two?!" LC said.

"Mom!" Little Sister yelled.

"All right, all right, what do you want?" LC whispered.

Little Sister looked around at LC's stuff. She smiled when she spotted the two baseball cards.

"I want those!" Little Sister announced, pointing to the baseball cards.

"No way! Not my rookie cards," LC said.

"Mom!" Little Sister yelled again more loudly.

"Yes, Little Sister?" Mrs. Critter called, coming to the doorway.

"All right, you can have one," LC whispered, flipping the Dizzie Dean Critter card over to Little Sister. There was no way he would let her have Hammerin' Hank. That was his favorite.

"What are you two doing?" Mrs. Critter asked, holding a plate of cookies. "Have both of you finished your homework?"

"I have," Little Sister said. "I had to draw a picture of my family. Here it is. Now I want to watch TV."

DADDY LC

"That's not home-work," LC said.

BABY "Is so," Little Sister said.

ME MOMMA

"I have *real* home-work," LC said. "*Thinking* homework."

"Did you finish your homework, LC?" his mother asked, putting the plate of cook-ies on the coffee table.

"Not exactly," LC answered.

"Then why don't you go upstairs and do your thinking homework at your desk," Mrs. Critter said.

Little Sister hopped onto the couch and fluffed up the pillows. She held the Dizzie Dean Critter card tightly as she picked up a cookie and took a big bite.

"Look, Mom," Little Sister said. "Look at this great card LC gave me."

LC rolled his eyes as he packed up his stuff. Little Sister didn't even know who Dizzie Dean Critter was.

LC walked slowly upstairs. He kicked open the door to his room. On the outside of his door was a sign he had made himself. It said:

KEEP OUT!
THAT MEANS YOU LITTLE SISTER!!!!

LC pushed a pile of stuff off his desk. Then he pulled out his math book. He looked around his room. There was stuff everywhere. LC meant to be neat, but he had too much stuff. He was always putting his things away but they never seemed to stay put away.

LC went over to the window and put some food into his fishbowl. Then he knocked on his spider's cage. Then he reached in to pet his frog. He looked back over at his desk. His math book was still sitting there.

LC plopped down on his desk chair and opened up his math book. He still didn't know how far TRAIN A had traveled. And forget TRAIN B. LC didn't like trains. They weren't cool. Surfing was cool. Why couldn't any of the math problems be about surfing?

LC thought for a minute. Then he drew a picture of two surfers on two surfboards.

LC
32

MALIBU MIKE 20

He labeled one "Malibu Mike" and wrote "20" under it. Then he labeled the other "LC" and wrote "32" under it.

And he figured out the problem.

$$2\tfrac{1}{4} \times 20 \text{ MPH} = 45 \text{ miles}$$
$$2\tfrac{1}{4} \times 32 \text{ MPH} = 72 \text{ miles}$$

CHAPTER 2

THE CHALLENGE

The next morning LC ate his bowl of Crispy Crispers cereal as fast as he could. He didn't want to be late for school. He put his empty bowl in the sink. "See ya," LC said to his dad, who was sitting at the kitchen table reading the newspaper.

"Have a good day," Mr. Critter said, looking up from his newspaper. "LC, can you stop by the hardware store

after school? They're holding a can of paint for me."

"Paint for what?" LC asked.

"For the new door I'm putting on the patio," Mr. Critter answered.

"Why don't you wait a minute for Little Sister?" Mrs. Critter said, walking into the kitchen.

"Can't," LC said. "Gotta meet Tiger and Gabby."

"I'll drop Little Sister off on my way to work, dear," Mr. Critter said.

LC slammed the back door and ran down the driveway.

Gabby was waiting for him by the mailbox. She lived next door. They'd known each other since they were babies. Gabby was tapping her foot and she had her hand on her hip. She wasn't smiling. LC knew that meant Gabby was mad.

"You are over two minutes late," Gabby said. "I almost left."

"Gabby, chill," LC said. "We won't be late." The two of them began to walk down the street toward school.

"But I promised Su Su I'd meet her at the lockers to talk about some stuff," Gabby said, her bracelet clinking as she walked.

"What kind of stuff?" LC asked. He was used to Gabby being very dramatic about everything. She wanted to be an actress when she grew up.

"Private stuff," Gabby said. "Girls only."

"Hey, did you see **KAYNE'S WORLD** yesterday?" LC asked. "That surfing competition looked really cool."

"How did you know?" Gabby said, stopping in her tracks.

"Know what?" LC asked.

"That me and Su Su are going to the Big Surf Competition this weekend and we're going to cheer for Slick Rick," Gabby blurted. "I mean, he is the—"

At that moment, something came flying out of the tree above them. Whatever it was landed smack on LC and knocked him to the ground.

"Gotcha," said Tiger, standing up. "Number One rule of the Ninja: Always be on guard."

LC stood up slowly. "Nice move, Tiger," he said.

"You two are soooo immature," Gabby said. "If you're going to do that stupid Ninja stuff then I'm not walking with you."

Gabby hurried off toward school. Her pink and yellow knapsack bounced as she walked.

"What's with her?" Tiger asked.

"She has to meet Su Su," LC said, kicking a rock with the toe of his sneaker. "They're making big plans to go to the Big Surf Competition this weekend. They're going to cheer for Slick Rick."

"Hey," Tiger said. "Some dudes have all the luck."

"Well, girls always like surfers," LC said.

"Yup," Tiger said. "Hey, did you see **KAYNE'S WORLD**?"

"Awesome," LC said. "Wish we could be in the Big Surf Competition."

"Yeah," Tiger agreed. The two boys ran up the front steps just as the first bell rang. They hurried over to their lockers.

LC's locker was right next to Gabby's. He opened the door as slowly as he could. But it was no use. All of his stuff tumbled out of his locker and fell to the floor.

"When are you going to clean up that mess?" Gabby asked LC. "I mean, we've only been in school for a week. And you've already trashed your locker."

"Really," Su Su said, nodding. Her pink surfboard earrings jangled up and down.

"Here he comes, here he comes," Gabby suddenly whispered. "Oh, Su Su, look how cool he is."

"Totally," Su Su agreed, following Gabby's eyes down the hall.

LC and Tiger looked at each other and then looked down the hall. Walking slowly in their direction was Slick Rick and a bunch of his friends.

"Hiiiii, Slick," Su Su said, batting her eyelashes.

"Hiiiii, Slick," Gabby said.

Slick simply nodded at the girls. Then he and his friends walked down the hall.

"Isn't he the absolute coolest?" Su Su said.

"Yes," Gabby agreed. "The coolest. And the cutest."

LC and Tiger made gagging faces at each other behind the girls' backs.

"What's so cool about him?" LC asked. He was getting a little bit tired of hearing about Slick Rick and how great he was.

"He's a champion surfer, that's what," Su Su said.

"Well, *I* surf," LC said.

"*You* do?" Gabby asked, her mouth dropping open in surprise.

"Well, yeah," LC said. "Doesn't everybody?"

"When did you learn how to surf?" Gabby wanted to know.

"I've been practicing all summer," LC continued.

"You have?" Gabby said.

"Yeah, and I'm pretty good," LC said.

"Oh, really," Su Su interrupted. "Well, if

you're so good then what competitions have you been in?"

LC didn't say anything. He didn't know what to say. He'd never been in any competitions. And he'd never surfed before. Ever. He'd opened his big mouth and said something without thinking. Now what was he going to do? He looked at Tiger.

"Well, LC . . ." Su Su said.

Su Su and Gabby stared at LC, waiting for him to say something. The second bell rang.

"I bet you don't even know how to surf," Su Su said.

"He does so," Tiger said suddenly. "In fact, LC has *personally* been invited to compete in the Big Surf Competition this weekend. Kayne *personally* sent him an invitation."

LC's eyes popped open wide and he stared at Tiger.

"Wow, LC!" Su Su exclaimed.

"How come you never told us that you surfed before?"

"Yeah," Gabby added. "That is *so* cool."

"Well, I don't like to brag," LC said.

The girls looked at him admiringly.

LC and Tiger grabbed their books and headed to homeroom. LC could hear Su Su and Gabby talking about him the whole way down the hall.

"Now what am I going to do?" LC said.

"Relax," Tiger said. "They'll forget about it. You know how girls are."

"You think so?" LC asked hopefully.

"Absolutely, dude," Tiger said, looking at LC. "Absolutely."

CHAPTER 3

SURFER DUDE

LC and Tiger met Gator, their other best friend, outside the cafeteria. LC was really looking forward to lunch today. It was Tex-Mex, his favorite. LC's mouth watered just thinking about the crunchy, munchy, delicious tacos.

As usual, Gator was already there. Gator was always on time. He was also the best basketball player in the school. He had a killer jump shot.

"Hey, dude," Tiger and LC said as they high-fived Gator.

"Hey, guys," Gator said as the three boys walked into the lunchroom. "Congratulations, LC! I can't believe you're going to be on **KAYNE'S WORLD**. That's excellent."

"What?!" LC and Tiger said together.

"What do you mean *what*?" Gator said. "Everyone's talking about it."

Tiger and LC looked at each other and then back at Gator.

"I think it's great, LC," Gator continued as the three of them moved down the lunch line. "You're like a celebrity already. I mean, since you're a top-ranked surfer and everything."

LC moved his tray along. He felt very

funny all of a sudden. And he had that weird jumpy feeling in his stomach that he got when something was very wrong.

"So, LC, are you really psyched?" Gator wanted to know.

"Psyched?" LC repeated, looking sick to his stomach.

"Yeah, about the Big Surf Competition and meeting Kayne and all that?" Gator said, picking up a container of milk and putting it on LC's tray.

"Hey, congratulations, dude!" a bunch of older kids said to LC.

"Can't wait till Saturday," one of the kids said, patting LC on the back.

"Hiiiii, LC," Su Su said. "Are you going to sit with us?"

LC nodded, but he didn't say anything. Things were totally out of hand. He had to do something quick.

"LC, do you feel okay?" Gator asked. "You look kinda green."

"No, Gator, I'm not feeling okay," LC whispered. "I have a big problem. Probably the biggest problem I've ever had."

"What?" Gator asked.

"He can't surf," Tiger explained in a low voice.

"But what about—" Gator began.

"It's not true," LC said. "None of it is true."

"You mean you're not a top-ranked surfer?" Gator said.

LC shook his head.

"And you're not going to be on **KAYNE'S WORLD**?"

LC shook his head again.

"Oh, really? That's too bad," Gator said. "Because everybody is really excited to see you in the Big Surf Competition this weekend."

"What am I going to do?" LC asked as he slid his tray along the line. He picked up a container of green Jell-O. Then he added two more to his tray. And then two more. And two more.

"Dude," Tiger said. "Since when do you like Jell-O?"

"I don't," LC answered.

"Then why do you have seven Jell-O's on your tray?" Tiger asked.

"Oh, no," LC said. "I told you I was in big trouble."

Tiger nodded in agreement.

"What am I going to do?" LC said again.

"You could always get sick," Tiger said, putting a large plate of tacos on his tray.

"Or you could just tell everyone that you don't know how to surf," Gator said.

"That's what I should do," LC said slowly. "Honesty is the best policy, right?"

Tiger, Gator, and LC paid for their lunches and walked toward the tables.

"Hey, champ," Henrietta said. She patted LC on the back so hard that he almost dropped his tray. Henrietta was in their class. She was the queen of the slam dunk. She also loved to eat. Last year she won the pie-eating contest for eating fourteen blueberry pies in fifteen minutes.

"Hope you beat Slick Rick

on Saturday," Henrietta said. She took a big bite of her egg salad sandwich. Yellow stuff squished out the sides of her mouth. "I'll be cheering for you, LC."

"LC, LC, over here!" LC heard a bunch of kids yelling.

"LC, we saved this table for you," Su Su said as she and Gabby waved their arms up and down. "Over here, LC."

LC followed his friends over to Gabby and Su Su's table. This was a perfect chance for him to tell the truth and get out of this surfing mess.

LC sat down slowly. Tiger and Gator looked at him. Tiger gave him a thumbs-up sign. LC cleared his throat. Gabby and Su Su were looking at him, too.

"You guys, I . . . um . . . sort of have something to tell you," LC began.

"Ooooh, isn't it soooo exciting!" Su Su said. "I can't wait till Saturday!"

"Really, LC," Gabby said, smiling at him.

"We're going to cheer for you, too."

"Um, guys," LC began again. "I have . . . um . . . something to tell you. . . ."

Just at that moment, Slick Rick came over to their table. He was with two of his friends. LC gulped.

"So, dude," Slick Rick said, looking at LC. "I hear you're a top-ranker. Cool."

LC gulped again. His mouth felt very dry all of a sudden.

"So, what kind of board do you use?" Slick Rick asked.

"Board?" LC said.

"I have a *Barracuda Z99*," Slick said. "It's real good on a free-fall. And it kicks out real well, too. What about you?"

LC didn't know what to do. Everybody was looking at him.

"I have . . . uh . . . a board you probably never heard of," LC said.

"Oh, you have one of those new ones? The experimental ones?" Slick asked, looking very interested.

"Uh . . . yeah," LC said. "It hasn't got a name yet. I'm really stoked about it."

"Cool, cool," Slick Rick said. "Can't wait to see it."

LC just nodded. He couldn't wait to see it, either.

"Well, see ya on Saturday," Slick Rick said. Then he and his friends walked away from their table.

"Yeah, see ya Saturday," LC answered. He picked up his milk, but he couldn't even drink it.

How could he have gotten himself into such a big mess? And how in the world was he going to get a surfboard by Saturday?

CHAPTER 4

THE SHARKBOARD

Timothy, Gator, Tiger, and LC were all in LC's clubhouse. It was really an old barn that used to be the Critters' garage, but LC and his friends had made it into their club.

It was Friday afternoon. They had less than one day to build a surfboard. Tiger had convinced Timothy, the class brain, to help them. Timothy said it was possible. He was a total science whiz and he had a photographic memory. He once built a radio out of crystals he grew himself.

"It's a simple problem of aerodynamics,"

Timothy said, looking up from a big textbook.

"Aero-*what*?" Gator, Tiger, and LC asked, staring at Timothy.

"What we have to do here is design a surfboard with the lowest drag coefficient possible," Timothy continued.

"Drag?" Tiger said.

"Yes, drag," Timothy said. "Drag is the force that retards the motion of the object moving through the fluid. In this case, LC on the surfboard is the object, and the water is the fluid."

Timothy stood and began to pace back and forth.

"Now, what in the ocean moves very, very fast?" Timothy asked.

"Fish," Gator said.

"Yes, but what fish moves like no other fish?" Timothy asked his friends.

"Uh . . . I know! A flounder," Tiger said. "They always swim away from my dad whenever we go fishing."

"No, no, no," Timothy said. "This fish eats flounders for breakfast. Think again."

Three faces looked blankly at Timothy. Timothy walked over to the blackboard at the back of the room. He picked up a piece of chalk and began to draw.

"A shark is one of the fastest fish in the ocean," Timothy said. "It has survived for millions of years because it is so fast. So, we are going to base our surfboard design on one of the fastest fish in the ocean. We are not going to build just an ordinary surfboard. We are going to build a sharkboard."

"Wow!" Tiger exclaimed. "Awesome!"

"What are you talking about, Timothy?" LC said. "We have less than twenty-four hours before the competition. How are we going to build any kind of surfboard, let alone a sharkboard?"

"By following the principles of science," Timothy answered. "Now, the first thing we need is a piece of wood. Not just any wood, but mahogany wood from the jungle."

"Mahogany wood from the jungle?" Gator repeated.

"That's right, mahogany wood from the jungle," Timothy said.

"Where are we going to get mahogany wood from the jungle in Critterville?" LC wanted to know.

"As a matter of fact," Timothy continued, "right here in this house there happens to be a very fine specimen of mahogany wood from the jungle. As I was walking in here I noticed there was a door propped up by your porch, LC. Do you know what kind of wood that door is made of?"

LC shook his head.

"That door is made of mahogany wood from the jungle," Timothy concluded.

"We can't use that door," LC said. "It's my father's new door."

"Do you want to win this competition or not?" Tiger asked, looking over at LC.

"Well, yeah," LC answered.

"Then we've got to do what we've got to do," Tiger said.

They followed Timothy out to the porch. Then they picked up the door

and began to carry it toward the clubhouse.

"Hey, what are you doing?" Little Sister yelled. "You better not touch that door! Dad will kill you!"

LC didn't even turn around. They were on a mission and there was no turning back.

CHAPTER 5

THE BIG SURF COMPETITION

Saturday morning was sunny and clear. It was a great day for surfing. Down at Big Surf Beach, Kayne and his camera crew were setting up. The competition was going to be broadcast live on TV.

The beach was jammed with kids and surfers. Everybody from LC's school was there. Su Su and Gabby were standing together. They were both wearing sunglasses.

"Doesn't Slick look so cool?" Su Su said, trying to see over the crowd.

"Yeah," Gabby said. "I wonder where LC is. He should be here by now."

"I bet he's not coming," Su Su said. "I bet he doesn't even know how to surf."

"He does so," Gabby said. "If LC said he's going to surf, then he's going to."

"We'll see, Gabby," Su Su said. "Oooooh, here comes Kayne. Maybe we can get on TV. Come on, Gabby. That would be the absolute coolest."

At that moment LC, Tiger, Gator, and Timothy were just rounding the corner, a block from the beach. They were all sweating and breathing hard from carrying the sharkboard. When they got to the beach, they dropped it on the sand and sat down to catch their breath.

Su Su and Gabby came running over. They both stopped short and stared at LC's board. Nobody said anything for a minute.

"That's a surfboard?" Su Su asked, staring at it over the tops of her sunglasses.

"It's not just a surfboard," Timothy said proudly. "It's a sharkboard."

"A *sharkboard*?" Su Su said. "Give me a break!"

"Yes, a sharkboard," Timothy said. "In fact, it is the first of its kind."

"That's no surfboard," Su Su said, walking around it. She took off her sunglasses to get a better look. "It looks like a door painted to look like a shark. I think it's really stupid."

LC's shoulders slumped. He wished he could disappear.

"Hey, dude!" Slick Rick called out, walking over to them. "Awesome board! Never seen one like it. Cool."

"I know, Slick," Su Su said, walking over to stand next to Slick Rick. "I was just telling them it was like the coolest board at the beach."

Just then a huge wave crashed against the shore. Everybody squealed as water

splashed everywhere. LC stood rooted to the spot. His eyes opened wide. He could not believe how big the waves were. They looked a lot bigger than they looked on TV.

"Monster waves," Slick Rick said. "Couldn't be better. Right, dude?"

LC nodded, feeling sick to his stomach.

Just then Kayne's voice came on the loudspeakers.

KAYNE: *Surfers, to the water. We're ready to rock 'n' roll. Get set for a truly rippin' time!*

"Follow me. I know the best takeoff zone," Slick Rick said to LC. "I'll show you where you can catch the biggest waves."

"Good luck!" Gabby and Su Su shouted.

"You'll need it," Tiger said.

"Thanks," LC answered. He picked up his sharkboard and dragged it across the sand behind Slick Rick. He didn't want the best takeoff zone or the biggest waves. He just wanted everything to be over. He wished more than anything that he was at home watching the competition on TV.

Back home, Little Sister was taking her bowl of Crispy Crispers cereal into the living room. She loved watching TV while eating her cereal. She was only allowed to do this on Saturday morning. And the best part was that she could watch TV by herself, without LC around to switch channels.

Little Sister picked up the remote and turned on the TV. There, right before her eyes, was LC at a beach with a whole bunch of surfers. He was dragging a surfboard into the water. Little Sister dropped her bowl of cereal.

"Mom! Dad!" Little Sister yelled. "LC's on TV!!!"

"LC?!" Mr. Critter said, running into the room.

"TV?!" Mrs. Critter said, right behind him.

Little Sister nodded, her eyes glued to the screen. All three of them watched in silence as LC paddled farther and farther into the water.

KAYNE: *Hey, dudes and dudettes! We're live from Big Surf Beach. And we're about to have the most rippin' surfing competition ever! We've got monster waves, and they just keep on comin'. It's an open invitational, dudes. Anybody can do it, if you're stoked and brave enough. It's the ultimate rush.*

Mr. and Mrs. Critter looked at each other. "LC doesn't know how to surf," Mrs. Critter said, looking upset.

"But he does know how to swim," Mr. Critter pointed out. "What I really want to know is where did he get a surfboard?"

"I know," Little Sister said. "He and his friends made it out of your new door."

"My new door?!" Mr. Critter exclaimed. "Oh, no! We better get down to Big Surf right away and find out what's going on."

As the Critters drove to the beach, LC paddled even farther into the water.

"Over here, dude," Slick Rick said to LC. "This is the ultimate takeoff. Where you are is for small waves. This is the best spot to catch the big ones."

LC gulped. He wanted to stay right where he was. He wanted to get the smallest wave possible.

"Come on, dude," Slick Rick said. "I'm telling you, this is the best spot."

LC paddled slowly over to Slick Rick. Slick was sitting up straight on his board,

his legs dangling in the water. He stared out to sea, trying to find the perfect wave.

LC was also sitting on his board, or trying to—the board was kind of wide and LC's legs were kind of short, so the board kept moving from side to side. It took a lot for LC just to keep his balance.

As the waves came in, surfers on either side of Slick Rick and LC paddled in toward shore to catch them. LC watched in amazement as the surfers stood up and rode the waves in to shore.

LC spotted a small wave. This was his chance to get back to shore and out of this mess forever. The wave looked almost harmless. It was a lot smaller than the other waves.

LC began to paddle.

"Dude, that wave's too small," Slick Rick said. "Take the next one. That's your wave. It's perfect."

Right behind the small wave was the biggest wave LC had ever seen. It was a monster wave.

"Go for it, dude!" Slick Rick yelled.

LC took a deep breath. He paddled furiously and caught the wave. He rode the wave to its crest. And then he stood up on the board as he began his free-fall.

Back on the beach, the crowd caught its breath. Kayne directed the camera crew to go in closer.

KAYNE: *It looks like the biggest wave of the day has been caught by an unknown surfer on an unknown board. The dude's got guts, for sure. But will he make it through his free-fall?*

"Who is Kayne talking about?" Su Su asked Gabby.

"I don't know," Gabby said. "I can't see."

"LC!" Tiger said. "It's LC! He caught the biggest wave!"

Gabby and Su Su pushed through the crowd to get a better look. And what they saw was LC crashing and tumbling through the surf. He wasn't standing on his sharkboard anymore. But he was holding tightly on to the doorknob as the board flipped over and over and bounced toward shore.

Gabby, Tiger, Gator, Su Su, and Timothy

ran down to the beach. LC and the shark-board had just washed up. LC had a dazed look on his face. Gabby helped him to shore as Tiger, Gator, and Timothy lugged the sharkboard away from the water.

Just then the crowd screamed as Slick Rick caught another monster wave. Unlike LC, Slick Rick rode the wave the whole way. The crowd cheered as Slick Rick kicked out the board and came running up on shore.

"Now *that's* surfing," Su Su said. "I knew you couldn't surf, LC."

LC sat in the sand. He was dripping wet, and there was sand in his shorts and in his mouth. He was miserable. He wished he'd never entered this stupid surfing competition. He wished he'd never even heard of surfing.

AND THE
WINNER IS...

"There he is!" Little Sister yelled, pointing and running toward LC. Mr. and Mrs. Critter lagged behind.

"You're really going to get it now," Little Sister said to LC. "You're all going to be in big trouble. Dad knows you took his door."

"Door?" Su Su said.

"Yeah, LC's surfboard is really our new patio door," Little Sister announced.

LC looked down at the sand. It was all over now. Everybody would know the truth.

"I knew that was a door," Su Su said. "I told you, Gabby. I told you LC didn't know how to surf."

"Shut up, Su Su," Gabby said.

"Well, he's no surfer," Su Su said. "He's a big phony."

Just then Slick Rick came running up to

them. He had his surfboard tucked under his arm and he was dripping wet.

LC gulped. Now even Slick would know he was a big phony.

"Excellent, dude," Slick said to LC. "Most excellent wipeout I've ever seen, dude."

"Yeah?" LC said, looking up at him.

"Yeah, you're really stoked, dude," Slick Rick said.

"You know, he never surfed before in his life," Little Sister said. "And that's no surfboard. That's our patio door."

LC's face fell. Now Slick would know the truth. He'd probably never talk to him again.

"Dude, you mean that was your first time?" Slick asked.

LC nodded.

"Well, you can surf with me anytime," Slick Rick said and smiled. "It takes a champ to catch the big waves."

"Yeah?" said LC.

"Most definitely," said Slick Rick as he high-fived LC.

Just then Mr. and Mrs. Critter made their way over to LC.

"LC, are you all right?" his mother wanted to know.

"Yeah, Mom, I'm fine," LC answered.

"That was a very dangerous thing you did, LC," his father said. "And you're

going to be grounded for ruining that door.
You'll have to pay for it."

"Sorry, Dad," LC said.

At that moment Kayne and the camera
crew came over to where they were standing. Kayne shoved the microphone in front
of Slick Rick.

KAYNE: *And now, here's today's champ, Slick Rick. This dude battled the monster wave and rode it all the way! Totally rad! And he gets a twenty-five dollar prize.*

The crowd hooted and whistled as Kayne gave Slick twenty-five dollars.

Kayne turned to LC.

KAYNE: *And over here, we have today's other winner. What's your name?*

"LC," LC said.

KAYNE: *LC, this dude over here, ate the big one and wins for most awesome wipe-*

out. And he gets a twenty-five dollar prize. Do you have anything to say to the **KAYNE'S WORLD** *viewers back home?*

LC hemmed and hawed. He couldn't think of a single thing to say. All he could do was wave at the camera. Then Kayne handed him twenty-five dollars and the camera moved off.

LC stared at the twenty-five dollars. He sighed and handed the money to his dad. It

was the least he could do.

Mr. Critter patted his son on the back. "Well, you definitely get points for trying,"

LC's father said. "Next time, ask first. Here's five dollars. You certainly earned it. Why don't you buy your friends some ice cream."

"Thanks, Dad," LC said. Then he turned to all of the Critter Kids. "Ice cream for

everyone!" LC said. "It's my treat!"

"Yay, LC!" the Critter Kids cheered. They jumped up and down and patted LC on the back.

LC smiled as he and his friends walked to the ice cream store. He couldn't believe he'd actually surfed. And he couldn't believe he'd won a prize. But most of all, he couldn't believe that he'd been on **KAYNE'S WORLD**!

It was awesome. Totally.